David Pelletier

The Graphic Alphabet

Orchard/New York

Orchard
95 Madison Avenue
New York, NY 10016

Manufactured in the United States of America
Printed by Barton Press, Inc.
Bound by Horowitz/Rae
Book design by David Pelletier
The text of this book is set in 24 point New Caledonia.
The illustrations are computer-generated images reproduced in full color.
10 9 8 7 6 5 4 3 2 1

Library of Congress Cataloging-in-Publication Data
The Graphic Alphabet/David Pelletier.
p. cm.
ISBN 0-531-36001-6
1. English Language—Alphabet—Pictorial works. I. Title.
PE1155.P45 1996
428.1—dc20 96-4001

For Hsien-Yin Chou, Luci Hitchcock, and
Zbyszek Kaluzka ~ who got me through it.   Thanks.

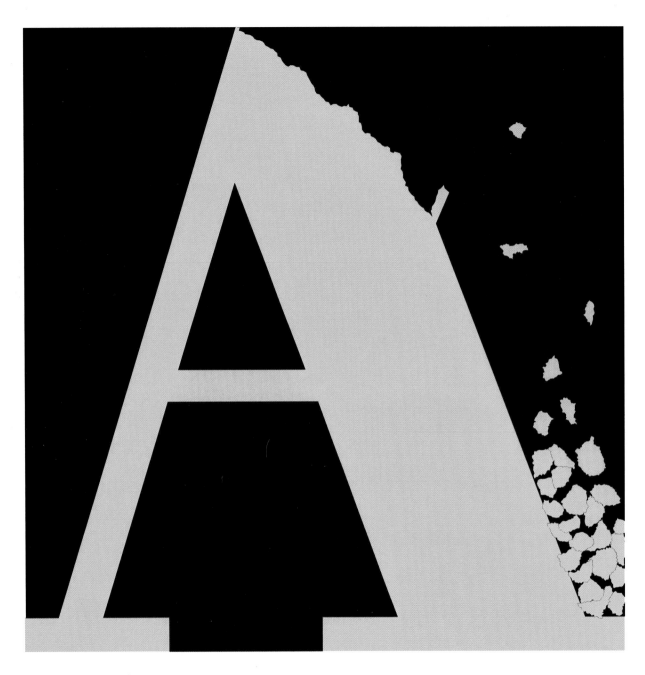

Avalanche

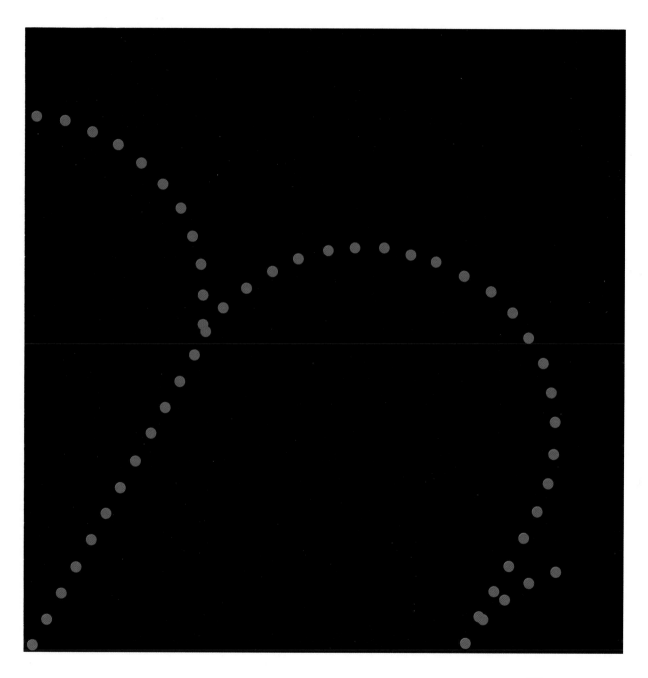

Bounce

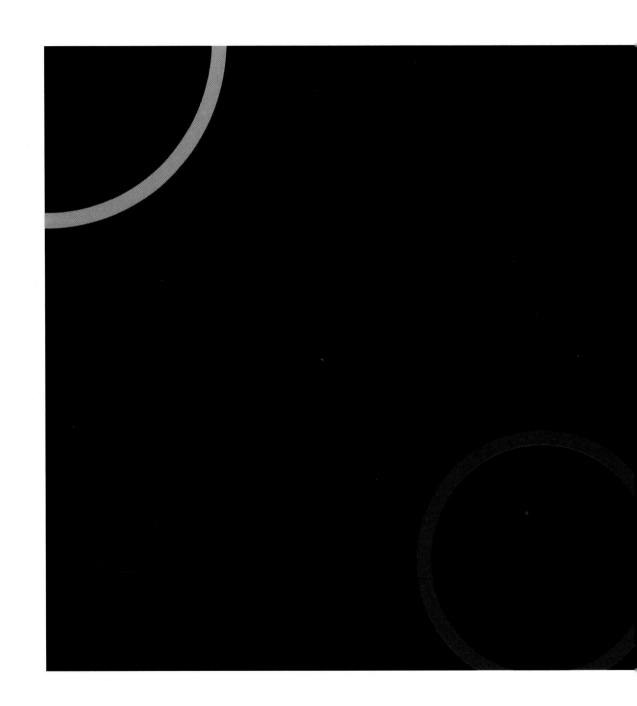

Circles

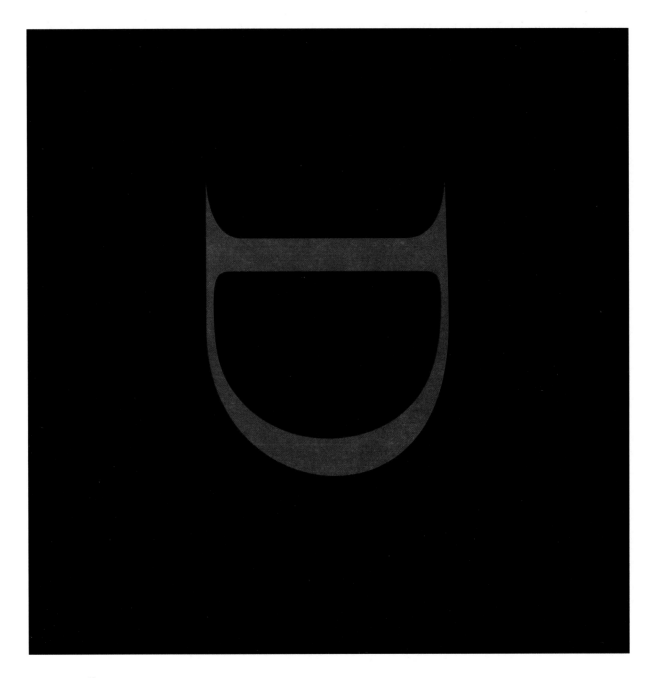

Devil

Edge

Fire

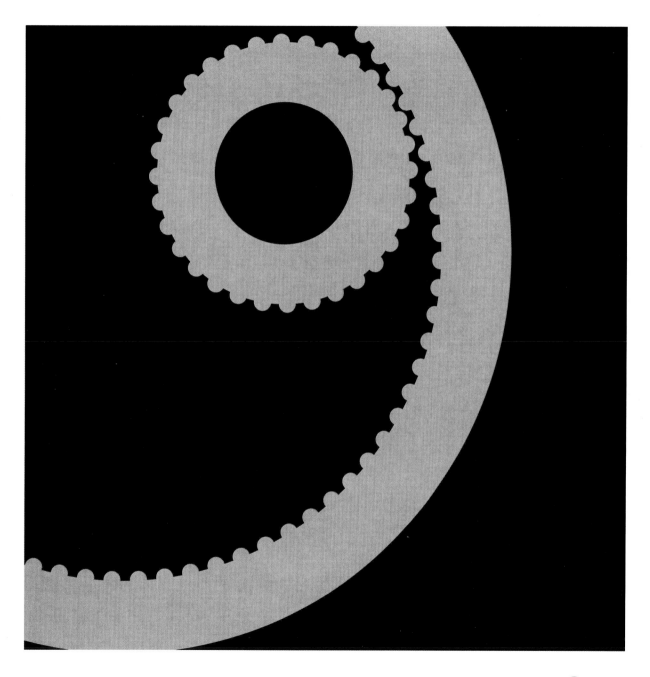

Gear

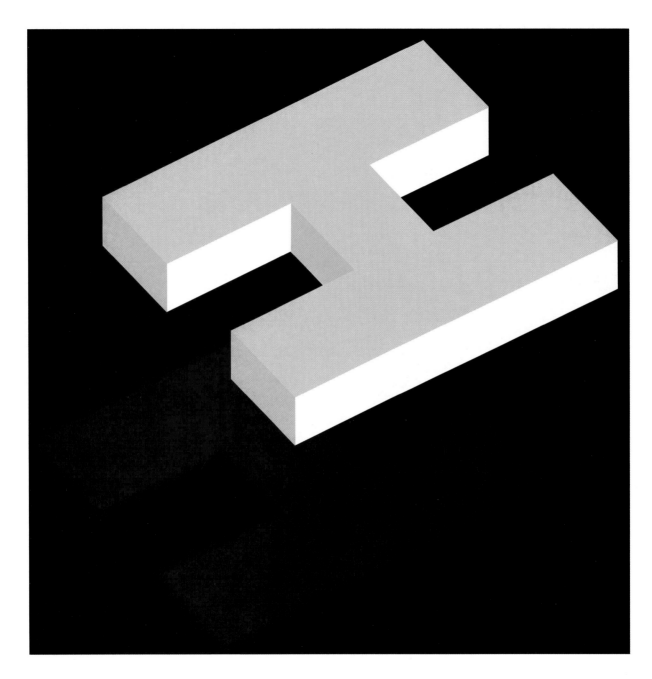

Hover

Iceberg

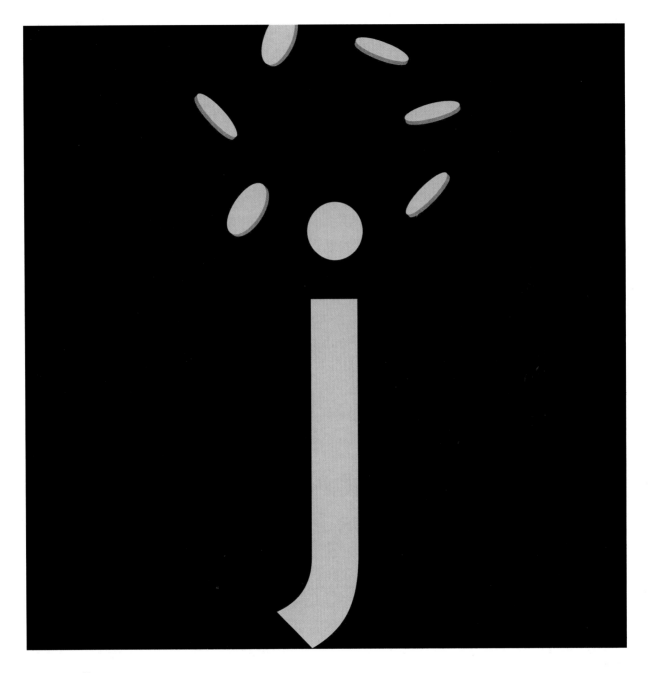

Juggle

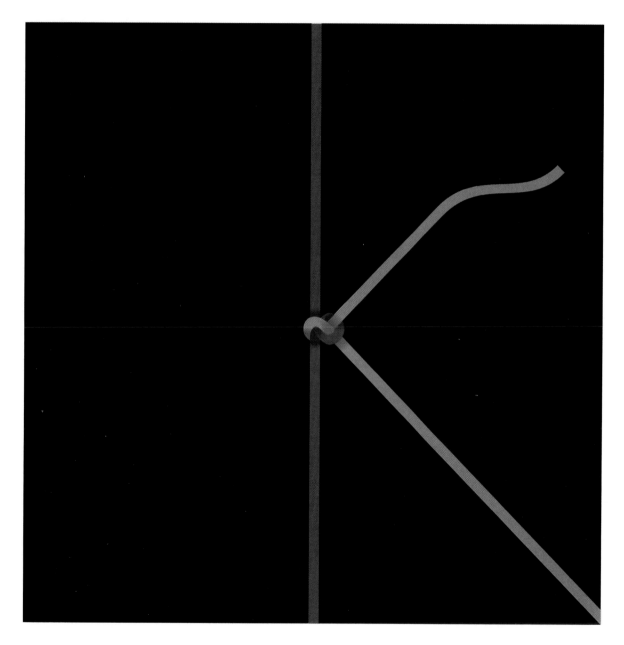

Knot

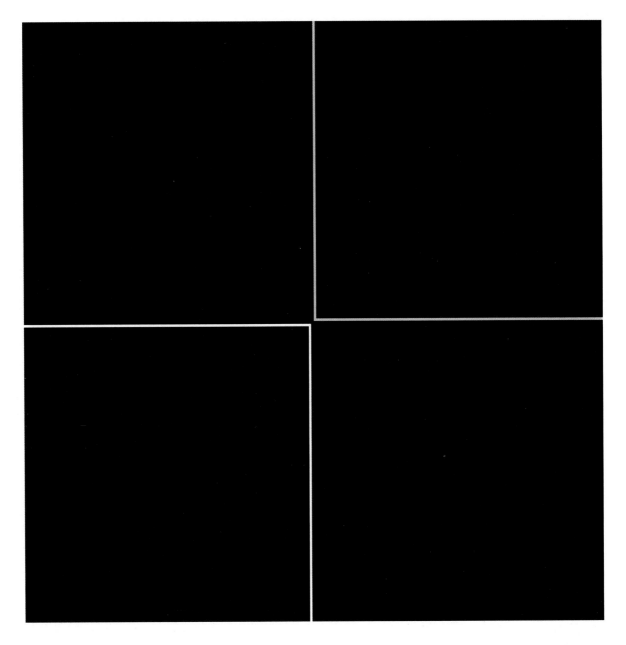

Lines

Mountains

Noodles

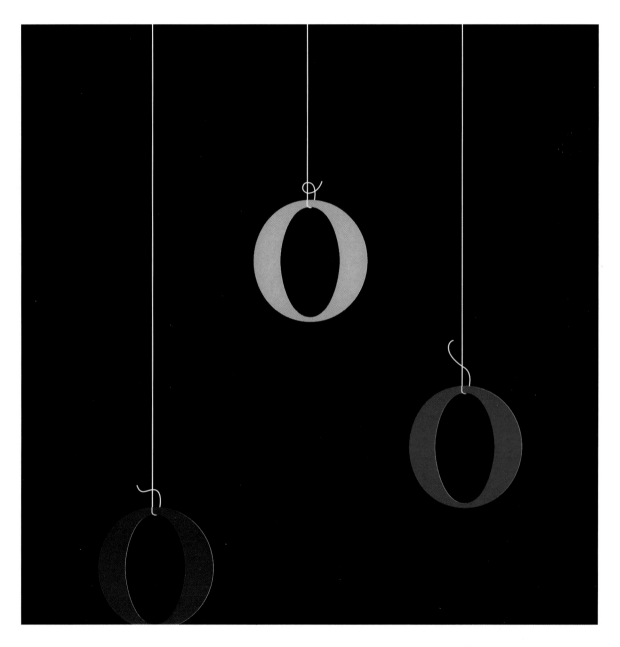

Ornaments

Pipe

Quilt

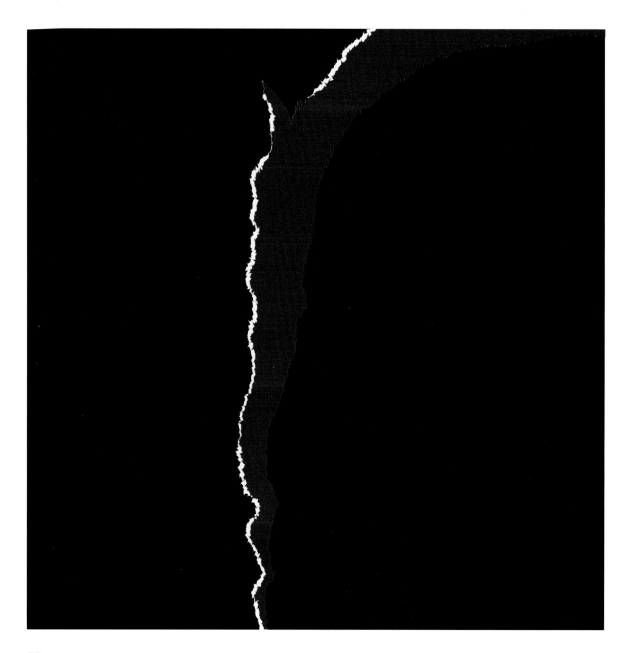

Rip

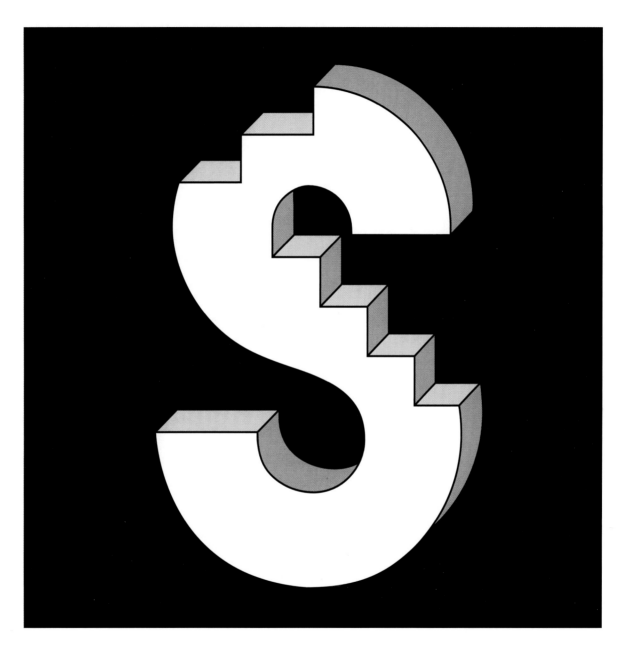

Steps

Trip

Universe

Vampire

Web

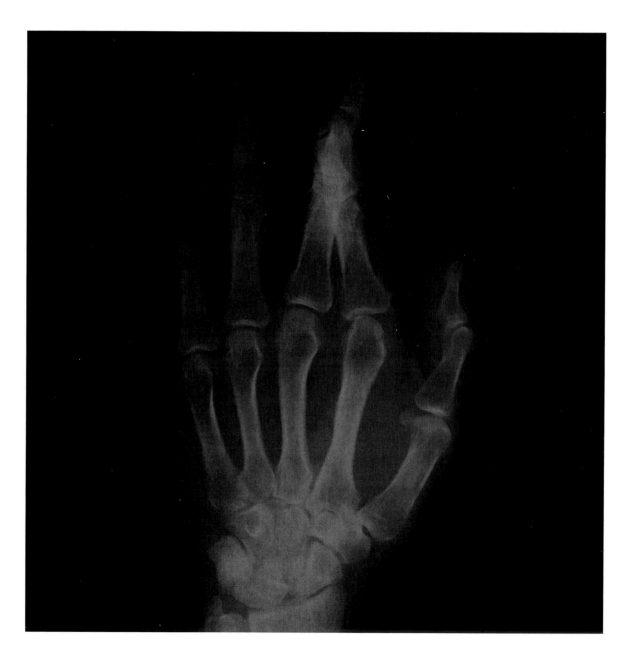

X ray

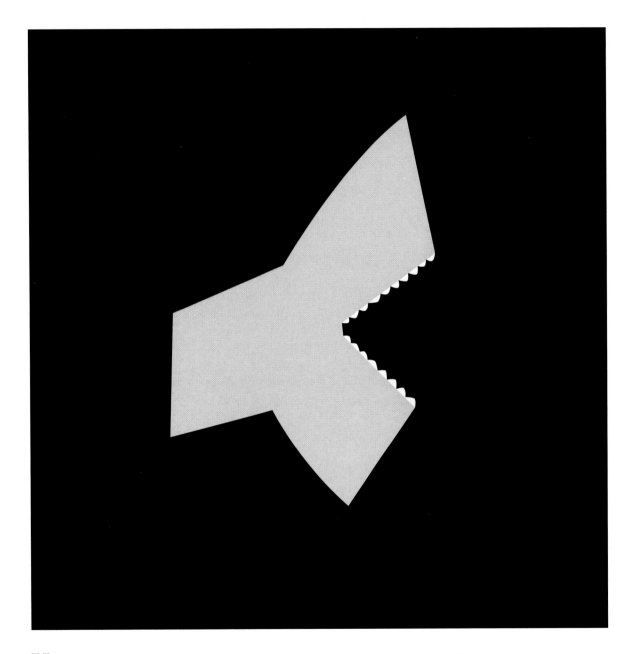

Yawn

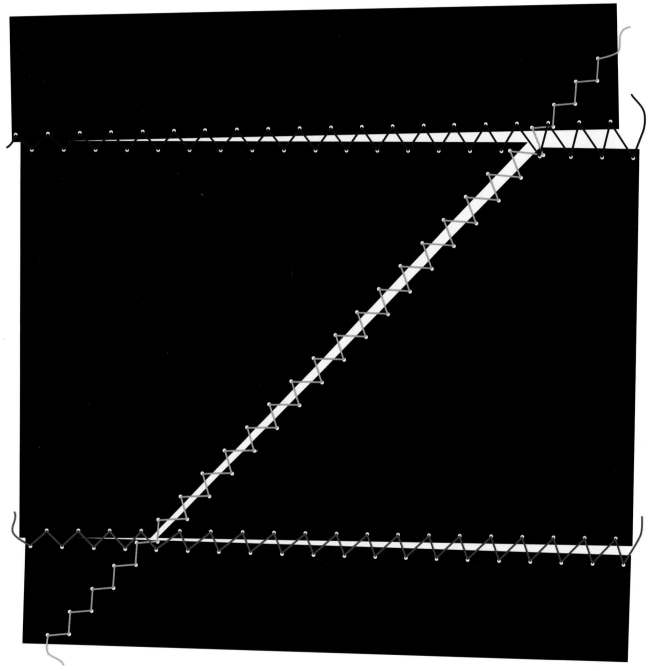

Zigzag